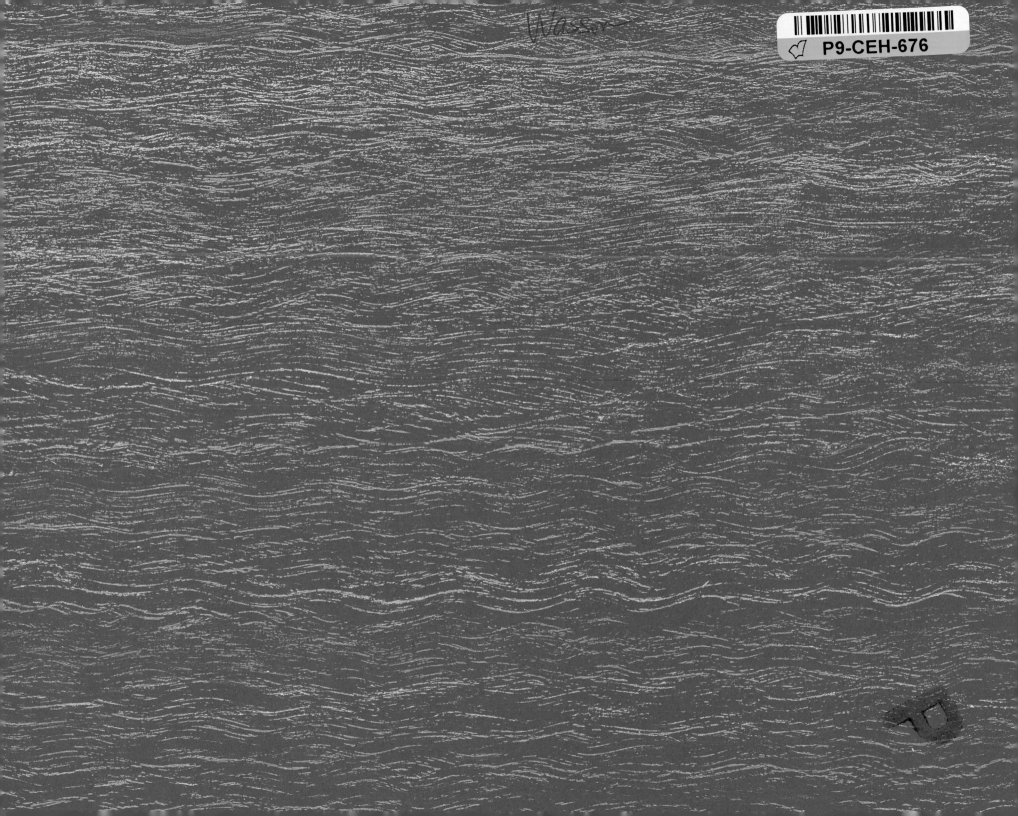

# BRIDGES ARE TO CROSS

PHILEMON STURGES

ILLUSTRATED BY GILES LAROCHE

G. P. PUTNAM'S SONS   NEW YORK

*To Lucy, Greer and Van - little bridges to a big future.*—P.S.

*To those who build bridges to bring people together.*—G.L.

G. P. Putnam's Sons, a division of The Putnam & Grosset Group, 200 Madison Avenue, New York, NY 10016.
G. P. Putnam's Sons, Reg. U.S. Pat. & Tm. Off. Published simultaneously in Canada. Printed in Hong Kong by
South China Printing Co. (1988) Ltd. Designed by Donna Mark. Text set in Berkeley Oldstyle Medium.
Library of Congress Cataloging-in-Publication Data    Sturges, Philemon. Bridges are to cross/
Philemon Sturges; illustrated by Giles Laroche.   p.  cm.   Summary: Discusses different kinds
of bridges, from train bridges to fortified castle bridges, and provides an example of each.
1. Bridges—Juvenile literature. [1. Bridges.] I. Laroche, Giles, ill.   II. Title.  TG148.S78
1998  97-13775  CIP AC  624.2–dc21   ISBN 0-399-23174-9
10  9  8  7  6  5  4  3  2  1  FIRST IMPRESSION

These three-dimensional illustrations were created on
a variety of paper surfaces through a combination of
drawing, painting, and papercutting.

**GOLDEN GATE BRIDGE**
*San Francisco, California*
Steel suspension bridge
1937

# Some bridges carry speeding trains across wide fjords.

---※---

### FIRTH OF FORTH BRIDGE
*Edinburgh, Scotland*
Double-cantilever steel bridge
1890

This bridge crosses an inlet of the sea to bring trains to the city. When first built, it was the largest steel structure in the world.

# Some carry llamas loaded with firewood across deep canyons.

**APURÍMAC RIVER bridge**
*In the Andes mountains of Peru*
Rope suspension bridge
Date unknown

This bridge is very old and very new. It was built long ago, but is always being repaired and rebuilt.

# Some let people dance over lazy rivers.

## STARK BRIDGE
*Stark, New Hampshire*
Protected wooden truss bridge
1862

Wooden trusses rot if they get wet. The cover is to keep the bridge—not the people dancing—dry.

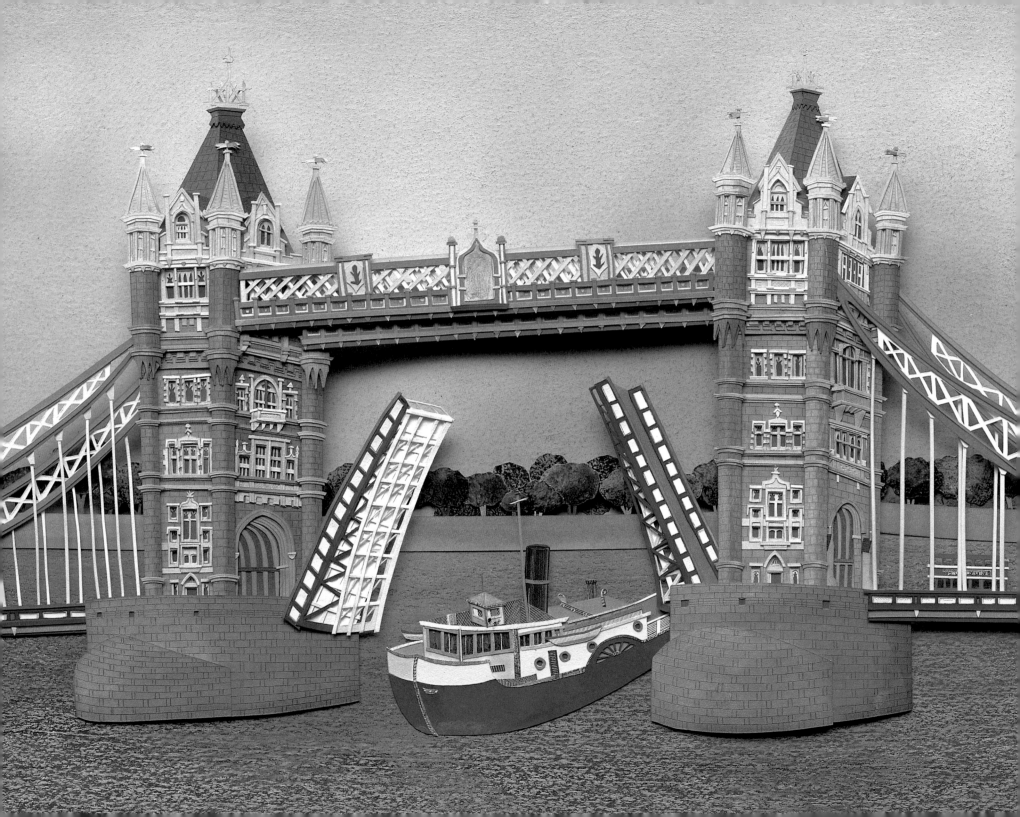

# This bridge lets boats float under the road.

**TOWER BRIDGE**
*London, England*
Drawbridge
1894

There are several kinds of drawbridges. Swing bridges pivot on a pier in the center of the river; vertical-lift bridges hoist the road up like a horizontal beam between two towers; and bascule bridges like this one have a hinged roadway that separates into two parts that swing up.

# This bridge lets boats float over the river.

CONOCOCHEAGUE AQUEDUCT
*Williamsport, Maryland*
Stone arch bridge
About 1835

In the days before railroads, barges carried heavy freight. They were towed by horses and mules in canals that usually ran alongside rivers. Waterway bridges called aqueducts carried canal water when they had to cross smaller streams or the river itself.

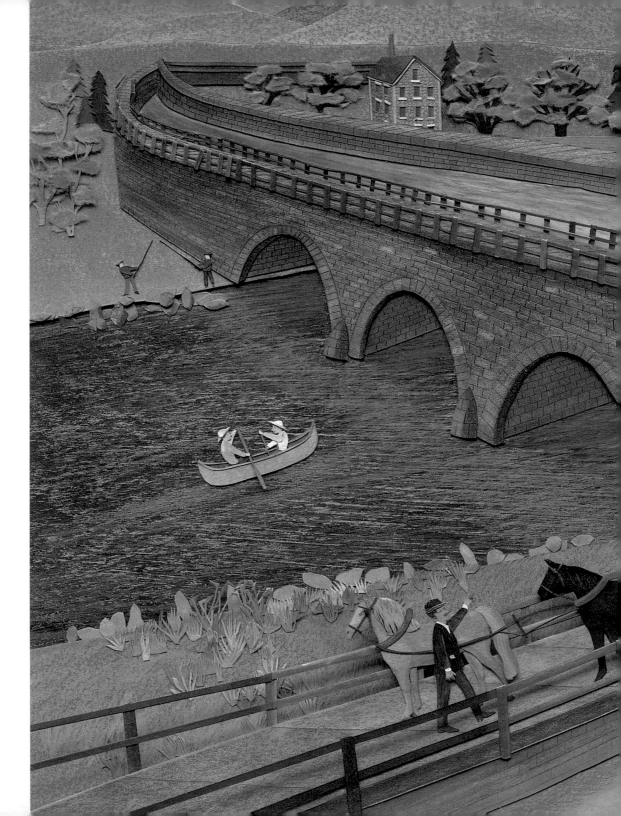

# And this one brings the river to the city.

———⚬———

## SEGOVIA AQUEDUCT
*Segovia, Spain*
Stone arch bridge
Probably first century C.E.

This is another kind of aqueduct. It was built by the Romans almost two thousand years ago. In spite of wars and earthquakes, it still carries water to Segovia.

This bridge was for emperors and popes to cross the swift Tiber River.

PONTE SANT'ANGELO
*Rome, Italy*
Stone arch bridge
134 C.E.

The Romans built this magnificent bridge to connect the tomb of their emperor Hadrian to the center of Rome.

A thousand years later the pope made the tomb into a mighty fortress. He topped it with a statue of Archangel Michael. Many years later other popes put a statue of a saint or an angel on each pier of the bridge.

# This bridge was for the shogun to cross to find the quiet of his garden.

## ENGETSU BRIDGE
Ritsurin Koen Park
*Takamatsu, Japan*
Curved wooden beam bridge
About 1600

The rulers of Japan crossed graceful bridges to islands in their gardens where they sat and thought, smelled soft air, heard fish splashing, and in the evenings watched the reflection of the full moon.

And this one's for
ordinary people
to cross, to shop, or
just watch gondolas.

—————⟩⟩⟩⟩—————

### PONTE DI RIALTO
*Venice, Italy*
Stone arch bridge
1591

Venice is made up of many islands separated by
canals, and since cars are not allowed, the bridges
there are to walk from island to island.

# Some bridges are forts to defend the castle.

———— ⟨⟩ ————

**PONT VALENTRÉ, CAHORS**
*Cahors, France*
Stone arch bridge
1308

The piers of bridges, like the bows of ships, face the flow of the river. This protects them from the swift currents of a flood.

Soldiers in the towers and battlements of this bridge protected it from invading armies.

# Some bridges are the castle!

—◆—

## CHÂTEAU DE CHENONCEAU
*Chenonceaux, France*
Stone arch bridge
1556

This was built by Catherine de' Medici, who married the King of France. She used it for splendid parties.

Later it became a place for artists and writers to share ideas, to paint, write poems, and compose symphonies.

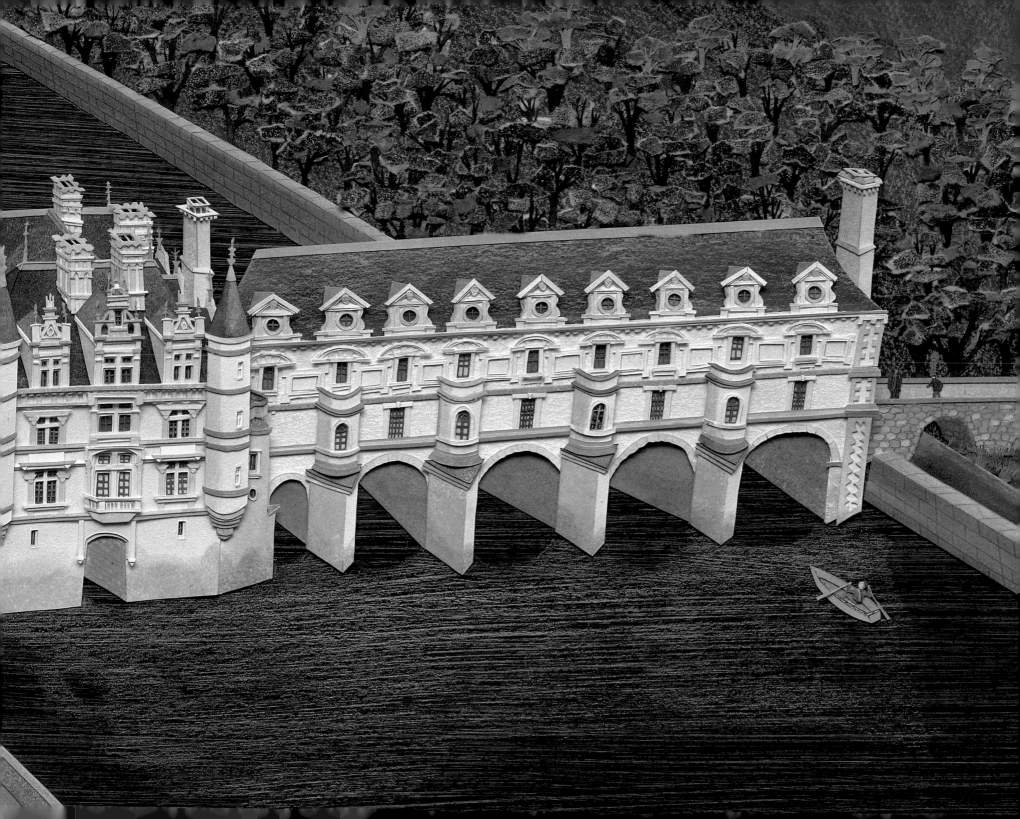

# This bridge spans a gorge on graceful concrete legs.

## SALGINATOBEL BRIDGE
*Schiers, Switzerland*
Three-hinged concrete arch bridge
1930

The two legs of the arch are shaped so that they are thickest where they would be most apt to break. The careful design made it possible to build a strong bridge that soars across the Schrau River.

# This bridge soars across Port Jackson inlet on a mighty steel arch.

———✦———

## SYDNEY HARBOR BRIDGE
*Sydney, Australia*
Bowstring arch bridge
1932

Here the roadway is hung below a giant arched truss. Notice the crisscross pieces, the cross-bracing, that keep the arch stable in the wind.

This bridge soars
across the East River
on woven webs
of wire.

———※※※———

BROOKLYN BRIDGE
*New York, New York*
Wire suspension bridge
1883

This bridge is like the Apurímac River bridge, but
bigger. Since the East River is not surrounded by
cliffs, stone towers were built to hold the twisted
steel wire cables. Here it is shown as it would have
looked in the 1880s, when its towers were among
the tallest structures in the city.

And this bridge just soars.
It carries dreams.